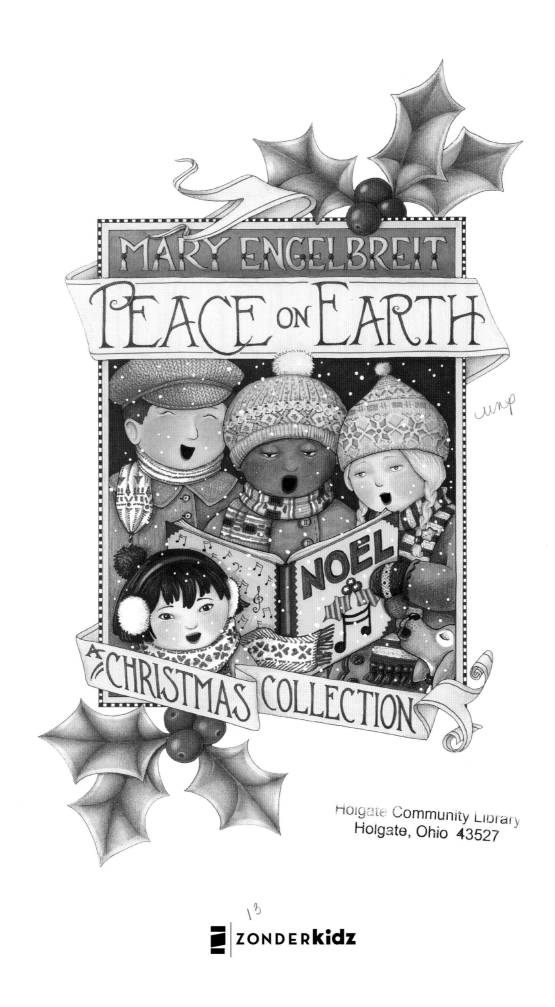

MARY ENGELBREIT

PEACE ON EARTH

NOEL

A CHRISTMAS COLLECTION

13

ZONDERkidz

WITH ALL YOUR HEART AND VOICE, REJOICE

ZONDERKIDZ

Peace on Earth, A Christmas Collection
Copyright © 2013 by Mary Engelbreit Enterprises, Inc.

Let There Be Peace on Earth copyright © 1955, renewed 1983 by
Jan-Lee Music, ASCAP. International copyright secured.
All rights reserved.

Requests for information should be addressed to:

Zonderkidz, 5300 Patterson Ave SE, Grand Rapids, Michigan 49530

ISBN: 978-0-310-74340-8

All Scripture quotations, unless otherwise indicated, are taken
from The Holy Bible, *New International Version®, NIV®.* Copyright©
1973, 1978, 1984, 2011 by Biblica, Inc.™ Used by permission. All rights
reserved worldwide.

Editor: Barbara Herndon
Design: Cindy Davis

Printed in China

13 14 15 /DSC/ 10 9 8 7 6 5 4 3 2 1

WE SHALL FIND PEACE.
WE SHALL HEAR THE ANGELS,
WE SHALL SEE THE SKY
SPARKLING WITH DIAMONDS.
···CHEKOV···

DEDICATED TO
MY MOTHER

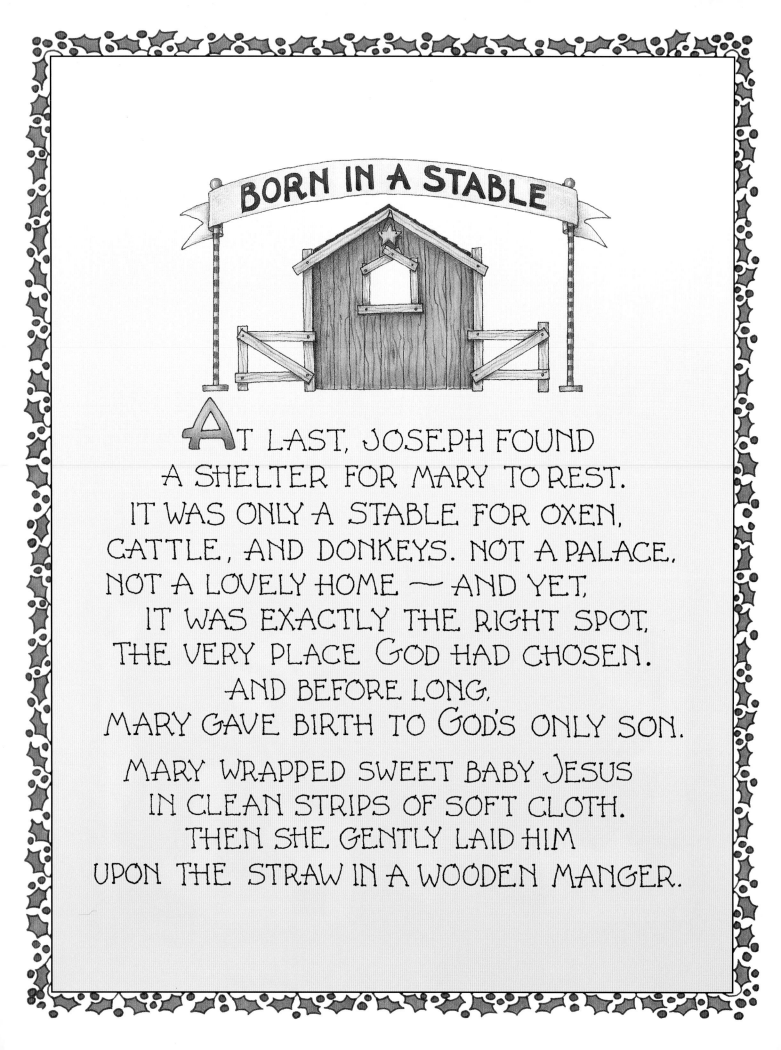

BORN IN A STABLE

At last, Joseph found
a shelter for Mary to rest.
It was only a stable for oxen,
cattle, and donkeys. Not a palace,
not a lovely home — and yet,
it was exactly the right spot,
the very place God had chosen.
And before long,
Mary gave birth to God's only Son.

Mary wrapped sweet baby Jesus
in clean strips of soft cloth.
Then she gently laid him
upon the straw in a wooden manger.

It should come as no surprise to you that Christmas is my favorite holiday. It's that time of year I'm able to decorate to my heart's content and indulge in the many traditions and rituals I grew up with as a child.

Over the years, Christmas books have been a big part of our family celebrations. The stories connect us to the spirit of the holiday as well as to one another. Many of the books given to me by my mother and grandmother were Christmas collections filled with stories, poetry, carols, and quotes. I have collected some of my personal favorites and included them in this book.

I hope the pieces in this Christmas collection inspire you as much as they inspire me. I believe they capture the true meaning of this wonderful holiday; a holiday that unites us in love and reminds us of the miracle of the season ... a small child, humbly born in a stable.

May this book speak to your heart and become a part of your own family's tradition for years to come.

Merry Christmas!

Mary

LOVE IS ALL

LOVE CAME DOWN AT CHRISTMAS,
LOVE ALL LOVELY, LOVE DIVINE;
LOVE WAS BORN AT CHRISTMAS,
STARS AND ANGELS GAVE THE SIGN.

- Christina Rossetti

PEACE is the rest of blessed souls. PEACE is the dwelling place of eternity.

Leo the Great

THE FIRST NOEL

The first Noel, the angel did say,
Was to certain poor shepherds
In fields as they lay;
In fields where they lay keeping their sheep,
On a cold winter's night that was so deep.

Noel, Noel, Noel, Noel,
Born is the King of Israel.

They looked up and saw a star,
Shining in the East beyond them far;
And to the earth it gave great light,
And so it continued day and night.

Noel, Noel, Noel, Noel,
Born is the King of Israel.

This star drew nigh to the northwest;
O'er Bethlehem it took its rest,
And there it did both stop and stay,
Right o'er the place where Jesus lay.

Noel, Noel, Noel, Noel,
Born is the King of Israel.

LOOK to THE BEAUTY of THIS DAY
MIRACLES ARE ALL AROUND YOU

THE GOSPEL OF ST. LUKE

And there were shepherds living out in the fields nearby, keeping watch over their flocks at night. An angel of the Lord appeared to them, and the glory of the Lord shone around them, and they were terrified. But the angel said to them, "Do not be afraid. I bring you good news that will cause great joy for all the people. Today in the town of David a Savior has been born to you; he is the Messiah, the Lord. This will be a sign to you: You will find a baby wrapped in cloths and lying in a manger."

Suddenly a great company of the heavenly host appeared with the angel, praising God and saying,

"Glory to God in the highest heaven, and on earth peace to those on whom his favor rests."

When the angels had left them and gone into heaven, the shepherds said to one another, "Let's go to Bethlehem and see this thing that has happened, which the Lord has told us about."

So they hurried off and found Mary and Joseph, and the baby, who was lying in the manger. When they had seen him, they spread the word concerning what had been told them about this child, and all who heard it were amazed at what the shepherds said to them. But Mary treasured up all these things and pondered them in her heart. The shepherds returned, glorifying and praising God for all the things they had heard and seen, which were just as they had been told.

DAY OF LIGHT · DAY OF BIRTH
HERE IS GOD
· COME TO
EARTH

THE DARLING OF THE WORLD IS COME,
AND FIT IT IS WE FIND A ROOM
TO WELCOME HIM. THE NOBLER PART
OF ALL THE HOUSE HERE IS THE HEART.

WHICH WE WILL GIVE HIM, AND BEQUEATH
THIS HOLLY AND THIS IVY WREATH,
TO DO HIM HONOUR WHO'S OUR KING,
AND LORD OF ALL THIS REVELLING.

Robert Herrick

FRIENDLY BEASTS

Jesus our brother,
Kind and good,
Was humbly born
In a stable rude,
And the friendly beasts
Around Him stood,
Jesus our brother,
Kind and good.

"I," said the donkey,
Shaggy and brown,
"I carried His mother
Up hill and down;
I carried her safely
To Bethlehem town."
"I," said the donkey,
Shaggy and brown.

"I," said the cow
All white and red,
"I gave Him my manger
For His bed;
I gave Him my hay
To pillow His head."
"I," said the cow,
All white and red.

"I," said the dove
From the rafters high,
"Cooed Him to sleep
That He should not cry;
We cooed Him to sleep,
My mate and I."
"I," said the dove
From the rafters high.

"I," SAID THE ROOSTER,
WITH THE SHINING EYE,
"I CROWED THE NEWS
UP TO THE SKY.
WHEN THE SUN AROSE,
I CROWED TO THE SKY."
"I," SAID THE ROOSTER,
WITH THE SHINING EYE.

"I," SAID THE SHEEP
WITH CURLY HORN,
"I GAVE HIM MY WOOL
FOR HIS BLANKET WARM,
HE WORE MY COAT
ON CHRISTMAS MORN."
"I," SAID THE SHEEP
WITH CURLY HORN.

"I," SAID THE CAMEL,
YELLOW AND BLACK,
"OVER THE DESERT,
UPON MY BACK,
I BROUGHT HIM A GIFT
IN THE WISE MEN'S PACK."
"I," SAID THE CAMEL,
YELLOW AND BLACK.

THUS EVERY BEAST
BY SOME GOOD SPELL,
IN THE STABLE DARK
WAS GLAD TO TELL
OF THE GIFT HE GAVE
EMMANUEL,
THE GIFT HE GAVE
EMMANUEL.

SILENT NIGHT

English lyrics

adapted from Joseph
Mohr's original German

Silent night, holy night,
All is calm, all is bright.
Round yon Virgin Mother and Child,
Holy Infant so tender and mild,
    Sleep in heavenly peace;
    Sleep in heavenly peace.

Silent night, holy night,
Shepherds quake at the sight.
Glories stream from heaven afar,
Heav'nly hosts sing Alleluia;
    Christ the Savior is born;
    Christ the Savior is born.

Silent night, holy night,
Son of God, love's pure light.
Radiant beams from Thy holy face,
With the dawn of redeeming grace,
    Jesus, Lord, at Thy birth;
    Jesus, Lord, at Thy birth.

A CHILD'S CHRISTMAS EVE DREAM

Ethel Van Deusen Humiston

Last night I had a lovely dream,
But strange as it could be,
For on the hill beside our house
Stood a great Christmas tree.

It glowed with lighted candles,
High at the top, a star,
And 'round it, dancing in a ring,
Children from lands afar.

There were polite, little English girls,
Swiss boys with funny skis,
Dutch children in queer wooden shoes,
Joined hands with shy Chinese.

Turkish lads in tassled fez,
Tots from France and Greece and Poland,
Laughing as the children do
In the safety of a free land.

Perhaps my dream's a prophecy
Of Christmases to be,
When little children everywhere
Can sing because they're free.

I surely wish with all my heart,
This day of Jesus' birth,
That peace and love and happiness
Soon cover all the earth.

"What means this glory round our feet,"
The Magi mused, "more bright than morn?"
  And voices chanted clear and sweet,
"Today the Prince of Peace is born!"
  "What means that star," the shepherds said,
"That brightens through the rocky glen?"
  And angels, answering overhead,
Sang, "Peace on earth, good-will to men!"

James Russell Lowell

THE MAJI

...And the star
they had seen when
it rose went ahead of
them until it stopped over
the place where the child was.
When they saw the star, they
were overjoyed. On coming to the
house, they saw the child with
his mother Mary, and they bowed
down and worshiped him. Then they
opened their treasures and
presented him with gifts of
gold, frankincense and myrrh.

Matthew 2: 9-11

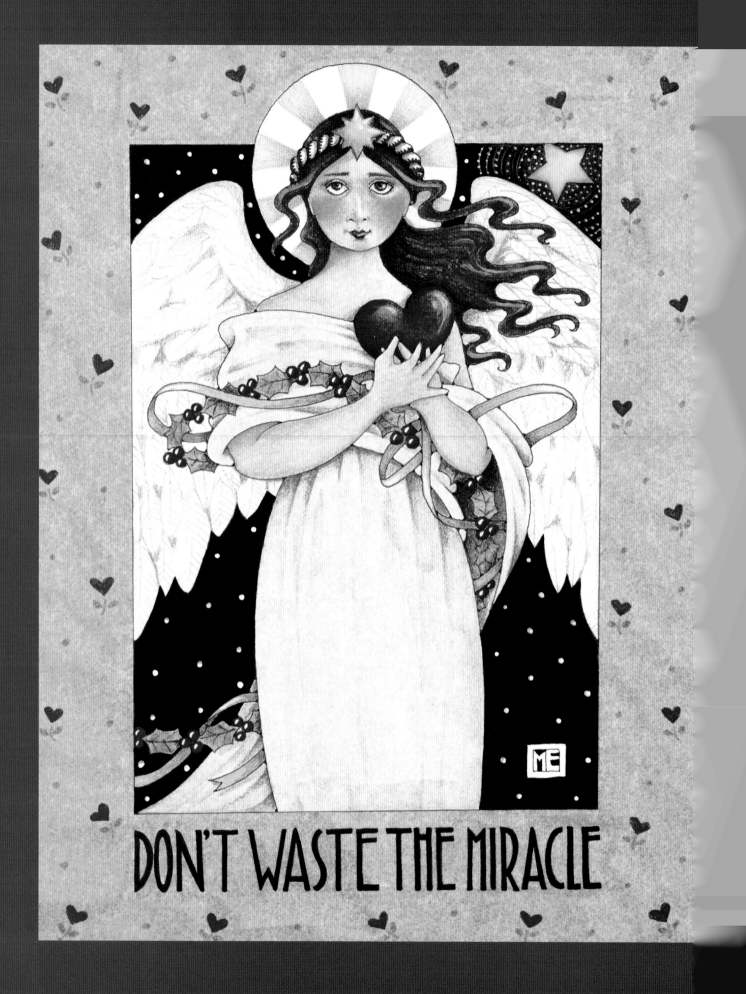

DON'T WASTE THE MIRACLE

DON'T WASTE THE MIRACLE

Jan Miller Girando

There's a miracle in Christmas—
there's a stillness in the air
And excitement in the shining eyes
of children everywhere.

There's a miracle in Christmas
as each silent night unfolds,
And we see again the promise
that this holy season holds.

There's a wonder in traditions,
in the stories passed along,
In our thoughtfulness toward others,
and in voices raised in song.

There's a reassuring comfort
in the joy glad tidings bring
And an inner peace from honoring
and praising Christ the King.

There's a magic in the season,
in the kindnesses we do,
Whether joys are shared by many
or among a special few.

There's awareness of our gratitude
for blessings from above;
There's a miracle in Christmas,
and the miracle is love.

Another Boy

The Story of the Birth at Bethlehem

Bruce Barton

Sleepless and bewildered but gloriously proud, the husband of Mary emerged from the stable and made his way to the census taker's booth. For it was the decree of Imperial Rome, ordering a general census, that had brought them to Bethlehem.

The angels' song hummed through his heart and timed his steps with its rhythm; his fine, bronzed face was radiant with the wonder of the night. But enrollment blanks and reckonings kept the census taker busy, and all he saw was another peasant standing in the line.

"Name?" he demanded in a routine tone.

"Joseph, carpenter, of Nazareth, of the house of David."

"Married?"

"Yes."

"Wife's name?"

"Mary."

"Children?"

The sturdy young carpenter drew himself up. "One child," he answered proudly. "A son, Jesus, born last night."

Was there any comment? Did the petty government official who wrote for the first time the name that was to be "above every name"— did he wonder as he wrote? Probably not. It was just one more name on the census roll. Just another boy.

What laughter would have rung through Rome if someone had pointed to that name and said, "There is the beginning of the end of your empire and of all empires everywhere." Yet it would have been true. Democracy began, and thrones began to totter when He said: "You are sons of God." For if all men are sons of God, then all are brothers, and the poorest are entitled to equal rights and privileges

with the King. Rome would have laughed, and Rome is dead. The influence of the Child lives on, uplifting the standards of action and thought, inspiring laws, enlisting the strong in service to the needy and the weak.

We celebrate His birthday, and the festival of all children everywhere. They, not we, are the really important people of the earth. In cradles, and at the foot of Christmas trees, are the lives that are to overthrow and rebuild all that we have built. Nothing is so powerful or so perfect that it cannot be transformed utterly by the miracle of another girl. Or another boy.

ANGELS WE HAVE HEARD ON HIGH

Angels we have heard on high
Sweetly singing o'er the plains,
And the mountains in reply
Echoing their joyous strains.

Gloria in excelsis Deo,
Gloria in excelsis Deo.

Shepherds, why this jubilee?
Why your joyous strains prolong?
What the gladsome tidings be
Which inspire your heav'nly song?

Gloria in excelsis Deo,
Gloria in excelsis Deo.

Come to Bethlehem and see
Him whose birth the angels sing.
Come adore on bended knee
Christ the Lord, the newborn King.

Gloria in excelsis Deo,
Gloria in excelsis Deo.

THE LAMB

William Blake

Little Lamb, who made thee?
Dost thou know who made thee?
Gave thee life, and bid thee feed,
By the stream and o'er the mead;
Gave thee clothing of delight,
Softest clothing, woolly, bright;
Gave thee such a tender voice,
Making all the vales rejoice?

Little Lamb, who made thee?
Dost thou know who made thee?

Little Lamb, I'll tell thee,
Little Lamb, I'll tell thee;

He is called by thy name,
For He calls Himself a Lamb,
He is meek, and He is mild;
He became a little child.
I a child, and thou a lamb,
We are called by His name.

Little Lamb, God Bless Thee!
Little Lamb, God Bless Thee!

ALL THINGS BRIGHT AND BEAUTIFUL

Cecil Frances Alexander

All things bright and beautiful,
All creatures great and small,
All things wise and wonderful,
The Lord God has made them all.

Each little flower that opens,
Each little bird that sings,
He made their glowing colours,
He made their tiny wings.

The rich man in his castle,
The poor man at his gate,
God made them, high or lowly,
And ordered their estate.

The purple-headed mountain,
The river running by,
The sunset, and the morning,
That brightens up the sky;

The cold wind in the winter,
The pleasant summer sun,
The ripe fruits in the garden,
He made them every one.

The tall trees in the greenwood,
The meadows where we play,
The rushes by the water,
We gather every day;—

He gave us eyes to see them,
And lips that we might tell,
How great is God Almighty,
Who has made all things well.

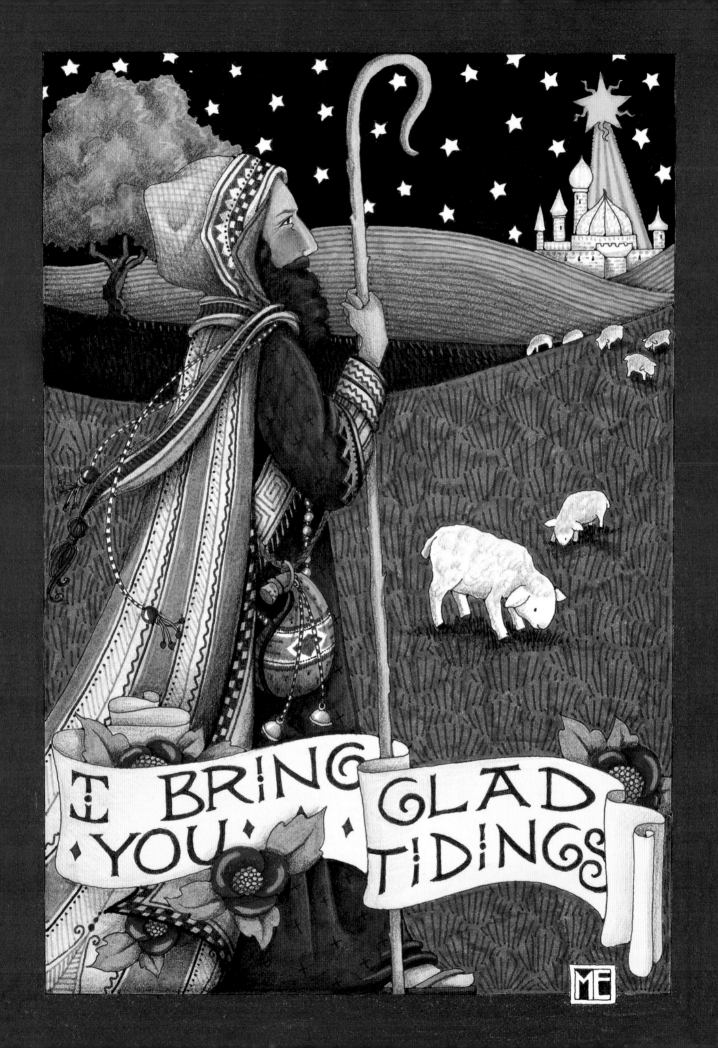

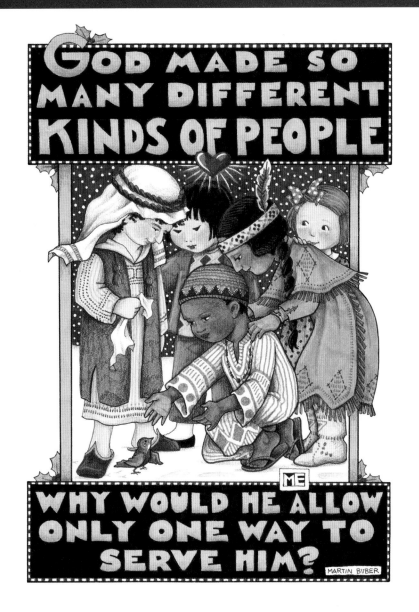

GOD MADE SO MANY DIFFERENT KINDS OF PEOPLE

WHY WOULD HE ALLOW ONLY ONE WAY TO SERVE HIM?

MARTIN BUBER

Let everyone be himself, and not try to be someone else. God, who looked on the world He had made and said it was all good, made each of us to be just what our own gifts and faculties fit us to be. Be that and do that and so be contented. Reverence, also, each other's gifts; do not quarrel with me because I am not you, and I will do the same. God made your brother as well as yourself.

He made you, perhaps, to be bright; he made him slow; he made you practical; he made him speculative; he made one strong and another weak, one tough and another tender; but the same God made us all. Let us not torment each other because we are not all alike, but believe that God knew best what he was doing in making us so different. So will the best harmony come out of seeming discords, the best affection out of differences, the best life out of struggle, and the best work will be done when each does his own work, and lets everyone else do and be what God made him for.

James Freeman Clarke

PRINCE OF PEACE

LET THERE BE
PEACE ON EARTH

By Jill Jackson and Sy Miller

Let there be peace on earth
And let it begin with me;
Let there be peace on earth,
The peace that was meant to be.

With God as our Father
Brothers all are we,
Let me walk with my brother
In perfect harmony.

Let peace begin with me,
Let this be the moment now;
With every step I take,
Let this be my solemn vow:

To take each moment and live
Each moment in peace eternally.
Let there be peace on earth
And let it begin with me.

LULLAY, MY LIKING

Anonymous

Lullay, my liking, my son, my sweeting.
Lullay, my dear heart, my own dear darling.

I saw a fair maiden
Sit and sing:
She lulled a little child,
A sweet lording.

He is that Lord
Who made everything:
Of all lords the Lord,
Of all kings the King.

There was much song
At that child's birth:
All those in heaven,
They made much mirth.

Angels bright, they sung that night,
And said to that child:
"Blessed be thou and so be she,
That is both meek and mild."

Pray we now to that child
And to his mother dear,
To bless us all
Who now make cheer.

Lullay, my liking, my son, my sweeting.
Lullay, my dear heart, my own dear darling.

IT CAME UPON THE MIDNIGHT CLEAR

Edmund Hamilton Sears and Richard Storrs Willis

It came upon the midnight clear
That glorious song of old,
From angels bending near the earth
To touch their harps of gold.
"Peace on the earth, goodwill to men,
From heav'n's all gracious King."
The world in solemn stillness lay
To hear the angels sing.

Still through the cloven skies they come
With peaceful wings unfurl'd;
And still their heav'nly music floats
O'er all the weary world.
Above its sad and lowly plains,
They bend on hov'ring wing;
And ever o'er its Babel sounds
The blessed angels sing.

For lo! the days are hast'ning on,
By prophets seen of old,
When with the ever-circling years
Shall come the time foretold.
When the new heav'n and earth shall own
The Prince of Peace, their King,
And the whole of world send back the song
Which now the angels sing.

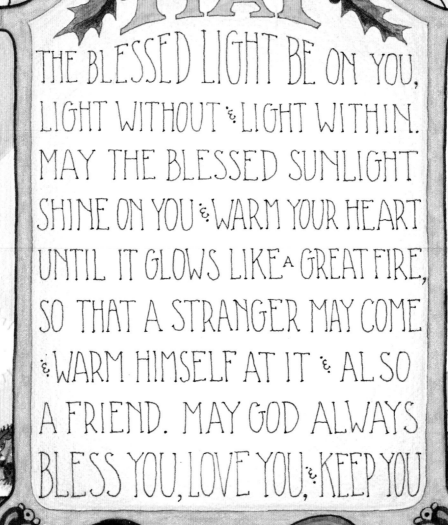

MAY

THE BLESSED LIGHT BE ON YOU,
LIGHT WITHOUT & LIGHT WITHIN.
MAY THE BLESSED SUNLIGHT
SHINE ON YOU & WARM YOUR HEART
UNTIL IT GLOWS LIKE A GREAT FIRE,
SO THAT A STRANGER MAY COME
& WARM HIMSELF AT IT & ALSO
A FRIEND. MAY GOD ALWAYS
BLESS YOU, LOVE YOU, & KEEP YOU